Storytime

For Mia Barclay and Esme Wren – G.A.
For Mum and Dad – M.B.

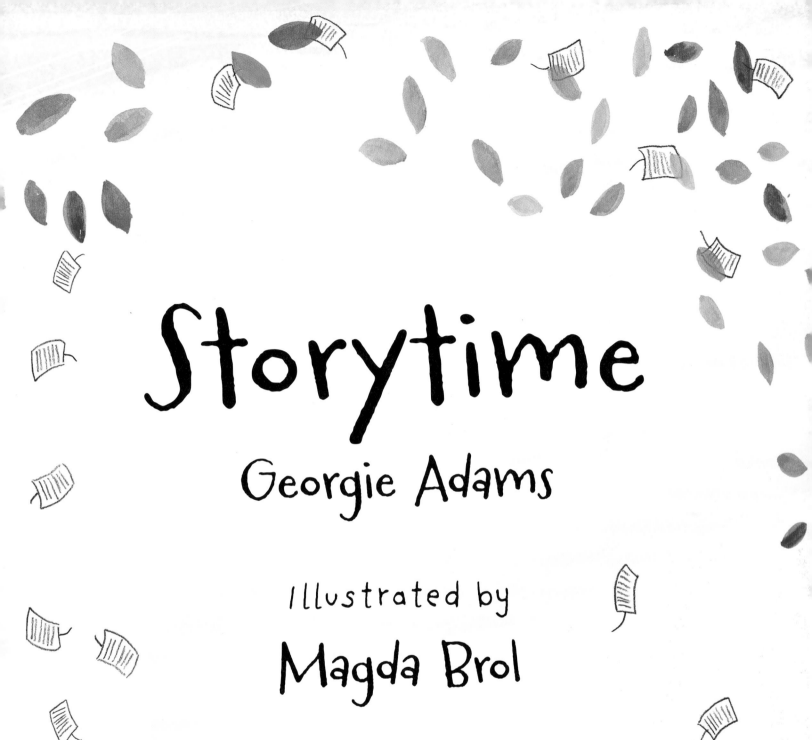

Storytime

Georgie Adams

Illustrated by

Magda Brol

ZEPHYR

An imprint of Head of Zeus

When I sat down to write these stories and poems I had super-busy lives in mind. Believe me, I know how tricky it is finding those few quiet moments in a hectic day to curl up and read a story! So I've mixed short, medium and longer stories to choose from — just right for reading aloud for whenever time allows — because sharing a story is the most precious time of all.

Easy-to-spot leaf symbols will help you to mix and match different stories and poems to suit whatever time you have:

short story

medium story

longer story

poem

Happy reading!
Georgie Adams

Contents

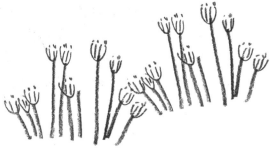

Step into Storyland and enjoy Storytime...

In Storyland, where Doogle, Buttons and Cabbage live, stories grow on the Story Tree. Every day they meet to read about their very own adventures, or something new. But one night a terrible storm blows all the stories away. The three friends set out to find them and bring them safely back.

We'll fly in my magic hat, of course. Even to the moon and back!

How will we get there?

Where shall we begin?

MAGIC WOOD

Buttons and the Humbly-Bumbly Bees

Once, I was in a hot, hot country, looking for Humbly-Bumbly bees. I'd heard they make the sweetest honey in the world and I wanted to try some. I was wandering along when I met a giraffe.

'Do you know where I can find the Humbly-Bumbly bees?' I asked. 'I've heard they make the sweetest honey in the world.'

The giraffe bent his long neck and looked at me with his big, brown eyes. He shook his head.

'I'm afraid I don't know.

Keep trip-trip-tripping along the track and you're sure to find them.

But be careful! Mother Tiger is about. She's looking for her cub.'

MAGIC WOOD

'A t-t-t-tiger?' I said. 'I'll try to keep out of *her* way!'

I thanked the giraffe and went trip-trip-tripping along the track, keeping a sharp look-out for Mother Tiger.

I came to a pool where some elephants were splashing about. A baby elephant squirted water all over me! It was a baking hot day and the water was cool, so I didn't mind. I asked the baby's mother if she could help.

'Do you know where I can find the Humbly-Bumbly bees? I've heard they make the sweetest honey in the world.'

The mother elephant thought for a moment and waved her trunk.

'I'm afraid I don't know. Keep trip-trip-tripping along the track and you're sure to find them. But watch out! Mother Tiger is on the prowl. She's lost her cub.'

'Yes, a giraffe told me about Mother Tiger,' I said. 'But thanks for the warning. My tummy wobbles just thinking about her!'

I set off once more trip-trip-tripping along the track, keeping my eyes wide open for Mother Tiger.

Soon I came to a jungle full of strange plants. I saw a monkey, swinging in a tree. I stopped to ask if he could help.

'Do you know where I can find the Humbly-Bumbly bees? I've heard they make the sweetest honey in the world.'

The monkey sprang down the tree from branch to branch.

'Hoo hoo hoo! I'm afraid I don't know. Keep trip-trip-tripping along the track and you're sure to find them. But be warned! I spotted Mother Tiger a short while ago. She's looking for her cub.'

BUTTONS AND THE HUMBLY-BUMBLY BEES

'Ooo-er,' I said, looking nervously over my shoulder. 'Yes, a giraffe and an elephant told me about Mother Tiger. My fur stands on end just thinking about her! But I've come all this way to find the Humbly-Bumbly bees, I can't give up now.'

I thanked the monkey and went trip-trip-tripping along the track, looking this way and that for Mother Tiger. I stopped suddenly when I heard a noise:

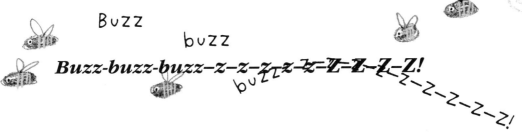

Buzz

buzz

Buzz-buzz-buzz–z–z–z–z–z–z–z–z–z–z–z–z–z–z–z–z!

I looked up and saw some bees, flying about at the top of a pom-pom tree. I recognised them at once.

'Hooray! Humbly-Bumbly bees!'

And in my excitement, I forgot about Mother Tiger.

I began to climb the pom-pom tree. It was a long way up. Luckily, when I reached the top, the Humbly-Bumbly bees flew away to look for food. They make honey from the nectar of gilly-gilly flowers. That's why it tastes so good!

When I was sure all the bees had gone, I looked inside their nest and saw a huge honeycomb, oozing with golden honey. I broke off a piece and took a lick. 'Mmmm!' I said. 'This *is* the sweetest honey in the world!' And I went on eating that lovely, sticky honey and didn't stop, until –

Buzz
buzz
buzz- z–z–z–z–z–z–z–z–z!

'Uh-oh. The Humbly-Bumbly bees are coming back!'
Quick as a blink, I put a small piece of honeycomb in my
pocket, then climbed down the pom-pom tree. It took me ages
because I was full of honey! By the time I reached the bottom,
the sun had set and it was getting dark. I felt very sleepy, so
I curled up at the foot of the tree and was settling down to
snooze when –

Thump, thump, thump!

I heard the unmistakable sound of paws –
big paws – thumping along the track.
Closer and closer.

And there, in the moonlight, stood…
Mother Tiger!

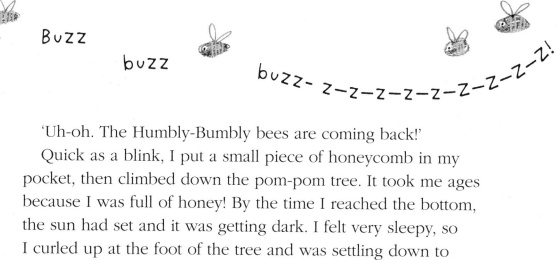

My tummy wobbled. My spine tingled.
I tried to run, but my legs wouldn't move.
Slowly Mother Tiger crept towards me.

Oh, *help*, I thought. *This is the end of me!*

Then she pounced.

'My baby,' she purred.

Before I knew what was happening, she
grabbed me by the scruff of my neck, and
carried me off through the jungle.

And the honeycomb in my pocket went
drip-drip-dripping along the track…

Mother Tiger took me to her den and
licked me all over. 'I thought I'd lost you
for ever,' she said. 'Where have you been?
Mmm! You taste of honey!'

Well, I was much too scared to speak.
Besides, her tongue was tickling my tummy!
It tickled and tickled. I tried not to laugh,
but I couldn't help it. Mother Tiger looked
very surprised and took a closer look.

'You're not my baby!'

She growled a terrible growl, curled her
lip, opened wide her jaws. I gulped and
shut my eyes.

'Please don't eat me!' I said.

BUTTONS AND THE HUMBLY-BUMBLY BEES

Just then, a tiger cub came bounding up.

'Mummy!'

Mother Tiger couldn't believe her eyes.

'*You're* my baby!' she said happily. 'How did you find your way home?'

'I followed a trail of honey,' said the tiger cub. 'It tasted so sweet I couldn't stop!'

I pulled the honeycomb from my pocket.

It's the sweetest honey in the world!' I said.

The tigers agreed.

'Thank you!' Mother Tiger said to me. 'You helped to bring my cub safely home.'

'Now it's time I was going home,' I said. 'Goodbye.'

So off I went trip-trip-tripping back along the track. On the way I saw the monkey, the elephants and the giraffe and told them the good news.

'Mother Tiger has her cub, and all because I found the Humbly-Bumbly bees who make the sweetest honey in the world!'

You were very brave.

You had a lucky escape!

Where to next?

Sweet Dreams

One evening, Sam's parents were going out and Mina had come to babysit.

'See you in the morning,' Mum said, kissing him goodnight.

'Behave,' said Dad, ruffling Sam's hair.

'Okay,' said Sam.

'Have a nice time,' said Mina.

Sam loved Mina. She could do magic!

'Will you do some tricks tonight, please?' he asked.

'Of course,' said Mina. She opened her magician's bag, put on a sparkly hat and took out her magic wand. 'Ready?'

Sam nodded.

Mina tapped the bag three times with her wand, muttered some magic words and – hey presto! – a bunch of balloons bobbed out.

'Wow!' said Sam.

There were more tricky tricks as Magician Mina turned six scarves into silky butterflies and pulled a furry toy rabbit from her hat.

Sam clapped and cheered.

'One more, please!' he said.

'Hmm,' said Mina. 'Let me think…'

She felt inside her sleeve, took out a coin and held it up for Sam to see. Then, with a click of her fingers – *poof* – the coin simply vanished.

'Where did it go?' Sam asked.

Mina pretended to look for it, until suddenly she opened her eyes wide.

'*There* it is!' she said, taking a shiny gold coin from behind Sam's ear. It was made of chocolate.

Sam quickly unwrapped it and took a bite.

'Yummy!'

Afterwards, he played a game on his tablet.

'What are you playing?' asked Mina.

'*Dragon Treasure,*' said Sam. 'I've nearly reached the dragon's cave. That's where the treasure is.'

But all too soon it was bedtime.

'Tablet off, Sam,' said Mina. 'PJs on.'

'Oh, just a bit longer, *please*!' wailed Sam.

'I'll count to five,' said Mina. 'One…'

'Count slowly,' said Sam.

SWEET DREAMS

'Two...' said Mina.

'Too fast!' wailed Sam.

'Three, four...'

'Stop!' said Sam.

'**Five**,' said Mina firmly. 'Off to bed.'

Sam pulled a face.

'I'll have to start all over again tomorrow,' he said.

'Never mind,' said Mina. 'Keep trying. You'll get there in the end.'

Mina read Sam a story, gave him a kiss and turned off the light.

'Sweet dreams, Sam,' she said with a knowing smile. 'Sweet dreams.'

That night, Sam dreamed he was on a daring quest to win treasure from a fierce dragon. It was just like the game on his tablet, only everything seemed real in his dream…

Sam peeped inside the cave. The dragon was sound asleep and snoring loudly.

z-z-z-z-z-z-z-z-z

With each tremendous snore, the ground shook beneath Sam's feet. Sam held his breath. Bravely he crept past the scaly, sleeping monster. And there – right at the tip of its tail – was a glistening pile of *gold*!

There was no time to lose. Quick as a flash, Sam grabbed a handful of coins. But, to his surprise, they smelled sweet – like chocolate. Strangely, at that moment, he thought he heard a familiar voice drifting through the cave: *Sweet dreams, Sam. Sweet dreams.*

Sam sniffed.

'Chocolate!' he said, unwrapping a golden coin and taking a bite. Then another. And another. He was just reaching for one more coin when, unfortunately for Sam, the dragon woke *up*!

The dragon opened one eye.

Then the other.

And the first thing he saw was – Sam.

Now, this particular dragon had a very sweet tooth. It made him red-hot, fuming mad to see Sam stealing his chocolate. With an ear-splitting roar and a blast of flames, the dragon blew Sam off his feet. Worse still, the dragon's fiery breath began to melt the chocolate.

'Time to go,' said Sam, picking himself up. Gooey chocolate trickled from the pile of coins, and Sam couldn't resist a last lick before dashing out of the cave.

Then he ran. He ran as fast as his legs could carry him and didn't stop till he was safely home in bed…

'Wake up,' said Mum, next morning.

Sam rubbed the sleep from his eyes.

'I found the dragon's treasure,' he said.

'Well done,' said Mum.

'It was made of chocolate,' said Sam.

'That's nice,' said Mum.

'But it melted,' said Sam.

'What a shame,' said Mum. 'Now, get dressed. It's time for breakfast.'

When Sam went to the bathroom he caught sight of a tiny trace of chocolate on his chin in the mirror. And he remembered the familiar voice he'd heard in his dream: *Sweet dreams, Sam. Sweet dreams.* That's what Mina had said last night.

'Wow! Mina really *can* do magic!'

Sleepy Sheep

Ten sheep in the kitchen,

Nine upon the stairs,

Eight sheep in the garden,

Seven are on the chairs,

Six sheep in the bathroom,

Five at my front door,

Four sheep on the ceiling,

Three more on the floor,

Two sheep on my bed,

One above my head…

Now,

Go to sleep, you sheepy-sheep,

It's time to go to BED.

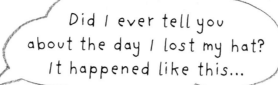

Did I ever tell you about the day I lost my hat? It happened like this...

Doogle's Flyaway Hat

I was out shopping one day when suddenly, a blusty-gusty breeze blew my hat away. It was my flippy-floppy-hat-with-a-bow-at-the-front-and-a-ribbon-at-the-back.

I ran after it. I chased my hat down the high street and around a corner. And there I met a dog called Dodo with stubby-short legs and a waggy tail. When Dodo saw my flippy-floppy-hat-with-a-bow-at-the-front-and-a-ribbon-at-the-back, he barked:

Bow-wow-wow

DOOGLE'S FLYAWAY HAT

'That hat looks fun to play with.' The dog called Dodo with stubby-short legs and a waggy tail ran after it too.

That blusty-gusty breeze was feeling playful. It tossed my flippy-floppy-hat-with-a-bow-at-the-front-and-a-ribbon-at-the-back into the air. It flew over a wall into a park. There we met an ooolly-ooolly bird with bright red wings and a yellow beak. When the ooolly-ooolly bird saw my flippy-floppy-hat-with-a-bow-at-the-front-and-a-ribbon-at-the-back, she sang:

'Ooolly—ooolly—oooh. That hat will make a fine nest.'

The ooolly-ooolly bird with bright red wings and a yellow beak flew after it too.

The three of us chased my flippy-floppy-hat-with-a-bow-at-the-front-and-a-ribbon-at-the-back out of the park. On and on we went, out of town and down a country lane.

There we met Mrs Go-Brightly and her bicycle with a ringly-tingly bell. She had stopped to pick blackberries, but had forgotten to bring a basket to put them in. When Mrs Go-Brightly saw my flippy-floppy-hat-with-a-bow-at-the-front-and-a-ribbon-at-the-back, she cried:

'Just what I need. That hat will make a good basket.'

Mrs Go-Brightly got on her bicycle with a ringly-tingly bell and rode after it too.

DOOGLE'S FLYAWAY HAT

Down the lane we went, chasing my flippy-floppy-hat-with-a-bow-at-the-front-and-a-ribbon-at-the-back. The blusty-gusty breeze was having such fun. At last we reached a farm.

In the farmyard we met Butter the billy-goat with his curly-whirly horns. When Butter saw my flippy-floppy-hat-with-a-bow-at-the-front-and-a-ribbon-at-the-back, he tossed his horns and said:

'That hat looks good enough to *eat*.'

Butter the billy-goat with his curly-whirly horns gave chase too.

Off we went across the farmyard following my flippy-floppy-hat-with-a-bow-at-the-front-and-a-ribbon-at-the-back. Soon we came to a cornfield.

In the middle of the field, we met a scarecrow with a tatty-torn coat and patchy trousers. His name was Harry. When Harry saw my flippy-floppy-hat-with-a-bow-at-the-front-and-a-ribbon-at-the-back he said:

'Oh! I've always wanted a hat like that.'

Then, believe it, or not, at that moment the gusty-blusty breeze blew away. And my flippy-floppy-hat-with-a-bow-at-the-front-and-a-ribbon-at-the-back fell from the sky…

…and landed on Harry's head.

'*Thank you*,' said Harry. 'It fits perfectly.'

I laughed to see the scarecrow so happy.

'You're very welcome to my flippy-floppy-hat-with-a-bow-at-the-front-and-a-ribbon-at-the-back. You need it more than any of us. You do a very useful job out here, keeping the crows away from the corn.'

Everyone agreed. So the dog called Dodo with stubby-short legs and a waggy tail, the ooolly-ooolly bird with bright red wings and a yellow beak, Mrs Go-Brightly and her bicycle with a ringly-tingly bell and Butter the billy-goat with his curly-whirly horns and I all went home.

But next day I went to the shop and bought a new one! It's my flippy-floppy-hat-with-a-DAISY-at-the-front-and-a-ribbon-at-the-back!

The Number Forty-Nine

People at the bus stop, waiting in a line,
for the bus to come along – the Number Forty-Nine.

There's –
A mum with her baby,
A young girl on the phone,
Two nurses dressed in uniforms,
A builder on his own;
A student with a double-bass,
A hiker and his pack,
Shoppers carrying heavy bags,
A burglar with a sack!

An artist with her easel,
An old man and his dog,
A tourist with a camera,
A schoolboy and his frog;
A family off on holiday,
A champion playing chess,
A football team with muddy boots,
A group in fancy dress –
All waiting at the bus stop, patiently in line,
but now it's here, so step aboard –
the Number Forty-Nine!

Cabbage Meets a Witch

I was dozing in the vegetable patch, under a cabbage. I'd been dreaming about a fat, flapping fish when something woke me. A rabbit was sitting in a row of carrots, crying. Big, blobby tears everywhere. For a moment, a flea-flitting moment, I thought about going back to sleep. I was snug and warm under my cabbage, and a cat needs his sleep, after all. But the rabbit looked so sad, I asked her what was wrong.

'My b-b-b-babies,' sniffed the rabbit, whose name was Frisk. 'That no-good Witch Mildew turned my babies into toadstools!'

'Why did she do that?' I said.

'For fun!' said Frisk crossly. She stamped the ground with her foot and made me jump. 'Mildew was bored so she cast a spell to amuse herself. She's always causing trouble. This time she's gone too far!'

'I agree,' I said.

I followed Frisk into Magic Wood where she lived, and she showed me six toadstools standing in a ring. At first, I thought they looked like ordinary toadstools. But when I looked more closely, I saw that each one had tiny rabbit ears. That set me thinking.

CABBAGE MEETS A WITCH

'It looks as though Witch Mildew's magic hasn't worked as well as it might,' I said. 'There's a chance – just a chance – I could change your babies back again. If only I could find a way to undo the spell…'

Frisk clapped her paws.

'Oh, please try, Cabbage!'

'I'll do my best,' I promised.

I left Frisk guarding her precious toadstools. I was deep in thought when I saw a fir tree – or something like a fir tree – wrapped in fur.

'H-E-L-P! PLEASE, HELP!'

A muffled cry came from the tree, so I stopped to ask what the matter was.

'That wretched witch!' said the tree. 'Mouldy Mildew, I call her. She tripped over one of my roots, so she cast a spell to punish me. "Call yourself a *fir* tree?" she sneered. "I'll show you what a *fur* tree looks like!" And here I am. Cocooned like a caterpillar!'

'Oh, dear,' I said. 'There's a chance – just a chance – I can find a way to undo her spell.'

The tree gave me a feeble wave with its branch.

'Thank you. Please hurry. I can hardly breathe inside this fur!'

'I'll do my best,' I promised.

MAGIC WOOD

I hurried on. By now, it was getting dark and Magic Wood was spooky in the moonlight. I was afraid I'd meet Mildew! But when I came to a river, I risked stopping. It was well past my supper time and my tummy was as empty as a bowl without milk. Luckily, there were fish in the river and I caught one in no time. I was washing my paws when I heard the strangest noise:

Ribbit, ribbit. Miaow!

A frog – or something like a frog – was sitting on a log, watching me. But this frog had a cat's tail and whiskers. After we'd introduced ourselves, Waffle, the frog-cat, explained:

'I'm the witch's cat. Or rather, I was until about an hour ago when I fell off her broomstick. Mildew took a sharp turn and I landed in the river. "Useless cat!" she shrieked and turned me into a frog. "Hop it and don't come back."' Waffle blinked a tear from his big, bulgy eyes.

'Ribbit, ribbit. Miaow!'

'Well,' I began, 'I think there's enough of you left to change you back again.' I told Waffle about the baby rabbit-toadstools and the furry fir tree. 'If only I knew how to undo her spells…'

Waffle leaped from his log.

'You need her spell book!' he said. 'It has a chapter on Troubleshooting and Undoing Magic.'

'Do you know where she keeps it?' I asked.

'Yes,' said Waffle. 'Mildew always tucks it under her pillow at night. She'll be fast asleep by now. Let's go!'

We hurried to Mildew's cottage and, sure enough, we found the witch asleep. My legs felt shaky as I crept to her bedside. I saw a corner of the spell book poking out, right by her nose! Slowly, very slowly, I slipped my paw beneath the pillow and pulled the book free.

Waffle watched me skim through the pages. I found the Troubleshooting chapter.

'Here goes!' I said.

A Spell to Reverse a Curse
(This spell works better
if chanted over a boiling cauldron!)

Hibble, Hubble, I smell trouble!
Cauldron boil and potion bubble.
Mischief magic is a curse,
Undo the spells – I say,

reverse!

Unfortunately, as I shouted –

'Reverse' – Mildew leaped
from her bed, wide-awake.

'How dare you steal my spell book!'
she screeched. 'Give it back!'

Mildew flew at me. She was quick,
but not quick enough! Before she could snatch the book,
I flicked it out of reach. Well, almost. Her pointy nails snagged
a page and tore it. Mildew lunged again. Too late! I'd flung
her spell book into the steaming cauldron.

Bubble, bubble. Fizz, fizzle, pop!

It was gone in a puff of smoke.

Mildew was fuming furious.

'You meddling moggy!' she snarled. 'I'll teach you a lesson.'
She aimed her wand, snatched up the torn page
from her spell book, and chanted:

'Curses on you, ever more,
You'll be a doormat on my floor!'

There was a loud *bang* followed by flickers of blinding, white light. We heard Mildew scream.

The curse hadn't worked properly because the page was torn.

Mildew's wonky magic had changed *her* into a *doormat* for ever!

Luckily, the reversing spell worked perfectly for everyone else. Frisk's baby rabbits bounced back as good as new, and the tree lost its fur. Waffle lived happily in the witch's cottage, and enjoyed wiping his paws on Mildew the doormat, every day.

As for me, I went back to my cabbage patch and slept till morning.

Let's hope we don't meet another witch. Come on, time to fly.

OVER THE RAINBOW

Rainbow's End

Knick-Knack and Know-How lived in a tree-house. Their home was made from findings Knick-Knack had collected, which Know-How had put together. It had a tin roof to keep them dry when it rained, and windows to let in the sunshine.

One day, a rainbow appeared above their tree.

'How pretty!' said Knick-Knack.

'They say there's a pot of gold at the end of the rainbow,' said Know-How.

'Treasure!' said Knick-Knack. 'Let's go and find it.'

'But where does the rainbow end?' said Know-How.

'I've no idea,' said Knick-Knack. 'But looking for it will be an adventure. We'll need a cart to carry our belongings.'

'We don't have a cart,' said Know-How. 'But I'll make one.'

Knick-Knack found
some planks of wood and
two wheels, dumped in a ditch.
Know-How nailed the planks together
and fixed them to the wheels. It made a
splendid cart. When everything was ready, they
loaded up and set off.

Rainbows come and rainbows go, but this one stayed.
Knick-Knack and Know-How took turns to pull the cart down
the road, following its arc of colours – red, orange, yellow, green,
blue, indigo and violet. Before long, they met a mouse who wanted
to know where they were going.

'To the end of the rainbow,' they said.

'Good luck,' said the mouse. 'I hope you find what you're
looking for.' The two friends travelled up hills and down dales,
and eventually came to the seaside. But they were no nearer the
rainbow's end than when they started.

'Look,' said Knick-Knack. 'The rainbow goes across the sea. We'll need a raft to follow it.'

'We don't have a raft,' said Know-How. 'But I'll make one.'

Knick-Knack collected driftwood and other useful things he found on the beach. Know-How roped the wood together and used a rag for a sail. When it was finished, they loaded up their belongings and headed out to sea.

The sky turned grey, though the rainbow remained bright and clear. Then came a rumble of thunder.

'Oh, no,' they said. 'There's a storm coming.'

A strong wind blew them into rough water. The waves got bigger and bigger! Up and down, up and down went their little raft. It made Knick-Knack and Know-How feel seasick. But they sailed on, until a whale popped its head out of the water and asked them where they were going.

'To the end of the rainbow,' Knick-Knack replied weakly.

'If we ever reach dry land,' sighed Know-How.

'Good luck,' said the whale. 'I hope you find what you're looking for.'

At last, they reached the shore on the far side of the sea. Knick-Knack and Know-How moored their raft. Their legs were wobbly after the voyage, otherwise they felt much better.

However, they were disappointed to find that they were no nearer the rainbow's end than when they started.

'Would you believe it?' said Knick-Knack, pointing to the rainbow. 'It's over that mountain! We'll need a hot-air balloon to fly there.'

'We don't have a hot-air balloon,' said Know-How. 'But I'll make one.'

Knick-Knack got busy looking for things to make a hot-air balloon. As luck would have it, he found an abandoned picnic basket. Inside were cups, plates and a patchwork tablecloth. Know-How knew just what to do. Using rope from the raft, he tied the cloth to the basket and made a canopy. Then he put twigs in a cup and lit a fire. Slowly, slowly, the heat from the fire filled the canopy with hot air.

When the balloon was ready to fly, Knick-Knack and
Know-How loaded up their belongings and cast off.

Up, up went the balloon, as high as the rainbow.

'Ooo!' said Knick-Knack as they drifted in a swirling mist
of red, orange and yellow.

'Aaah!' said Know-How as they floated through wisps of
green, blue, indigo and violet.

They glided in a cloud of colours, till they sailed right
over the mountain. But still the rainbow didn't end there.
It seemed to be never-ending! Knick-Knack and
Know-How were wondering what to do, when
an eagle flew by and wanted to know where
they were going.

'We're looking for the end of the rainbow,' they said.

'Good luck,' said the eagle. 'I hope you find what you're looking for.'

A moment later, the fire went out. The air in the canopy cooled and the balloon began to shrink.

'Oh, no!' cried Knick-Knack.

'Hold on tight. We're going down,' said Know-How.

But the balloon didn't fall. Instead, it glided smoothly along the arc of the rainbow, high across the mountain, back across the sea, over the hills and dales, and the road where their journey had begun. Then – *bump*. They landed gently beside their very own tree-house.

Knick-Knack and Know-How jumped out.

'So *this* is where the rainbow ends!' said Knick-Knack.

'Who wants treasure anyway?' said Know-How. 'We have everything we need right here.'

And they agreed that home was exactly what they were looking for and never chased rainbows again.

A Holiday to Remember

Frankie lived in a city with her parents and her dog, Mops. Ever since they'd brought the mischievous mongrel home from an animal rescue centre, Frankie and Mops had been inseparable.

When Frankie's mum, Alex, announced they were going on holiday, the first thing Frankie said was:

'Can Mops come too?'

Mops gazed at Frankie lovingly and wagged his tail, fast.

'He'll be good!' she said, hugging him. 'It's not his fault he hates loud noises. Where are we going?'

'We've booked a nice quiet cottage in the country,' said Alex.

Frankie groaned.

'There's nothing to do in the country. Sooooo boring!'

Just then Alex's phone rang and she answered it immediately.

'I'm on my way,' she said.

Frankie was used to her parents dashing off at odd times of the day or night. Her mum was a paramedic on call to attend anyone in urgent need of medical attention. She rode a specially-equipped motorbike and could weave in and out of traffic faster than an ambulance.

Frankie's dad was a busy detective with the city police force. *No wonder they want a quiet holiday in the country,* thought Frankie.

A HOLIDAY TO REMEMBER

It was a long journey to the cottage, and Frankie's parents took turns to drive. For a while she stared out of the car window; streets, shops, tower blocks, houses and factories whizzed by. Gradually these gave way to villages, woods and fields. Mops slept most of the way. It was late, pouring with rain and too dark to see anything when they reached the cottage. After a hasty supper, everyone went to bed.

Next morning, Frankie was woken by Mops whining to go out. She ran downstairs and opened the door. It had stopped raining, but there were puddles everywhere. Frankie pulled on her boots and stepped outside, still wearing her PJs. Mops made straight for the biggest puddle, barking madly.

Pete and Alex came hurrying to see what was going on.

'It's so early,' said Alex, yawning. 'We're supposed to be on holiday!'

But Frankie wasn't listening. She'd spotted something amazing.

'Mum. Dad. Look. Donkeys. Lots and lots of donkeys!'

'Oh, didn't we say?' said her dad. 'We booked a cottage next to a donkey sanctuary. We'll go there after breakfast.'

Frankie couldn't stop smiling.

OVER THE RAINBOW

Frankie and her parents met Rachel, the farmer who also ran Rainbow's End Donkey Sanctuary. She made a fuss of Mops.

'You're a lovely boy. And wearing a nice new collar and lead. It's best to keep dogs under control around farm animals. Especially our rescue donkeys.'

She took them into a yard where there were stables with names on the doors:

'Bumble, Florence, Dennis and Molly,' Frankie read aloud.

'We usually keep our new arrivals stabled,' Rachel explained, 'until they're ready to go out with the others. Some donkeys arrive in very poor condition. People can be so cruel—'

'I know!' cried Frankie. 'Mops was badly treated as a puppy. We got him from a rescue place.'

'He's a lucky dog,' said Rachel. 'I can tell you love animals.'

'I want to be a vet when I grow up,' said Frankie.

'I'm sure you'll make a good one,' said Rachel. 'Our vet Nikki is coming to see Florence tomorrow. She hasn't been eating properly. Would you like to watch Nikki at work?'

'Yes, please,' said Frankie.

BUMBLE

DENNIS

The week flew by faster than Frankie could have imagined was possible. There was always so much to do. Frankie fed the donkeys, mucked out stables and groomed. Rachel taught her about donkeys too.

'You can tell how a donkey is feeling by looking at its ears,' she said. 'Florence loves being brushed, and I'm pleased to say she's eating properly again. Nikki knew how to treat her.'

On the last day of the holiday, Rachel's son, Dillon, who was in charge of the farm animals, roared by on his big, red tractor.

A HOLIDAY TO REMEMBER

Mops barked excitedly. Frankie held tight to his lead.

'Dillon drives too fast!' said Rachel. 'I've warned him to slow down.'

The tractor was carrying an enormous bale of hay.

'It's for our herd of dairy cows,' said Rachel. 'Sometimes there's not quite enough grass for them. So we give them extra food. We have a flock of sheep and free-range hens. Let's collect some eggs and you can have them for tea.'

As Frankie was carrying eggs back to the cottage it started to rain –
even though the sun was still shining. Suddenly, a flash of lightning
lit up the sky. Mops whimpered. *Boom* – a thunderclap crashed
overhead. Mops yanked the lead from Frankie's grasp and took off.
She dropped the eggs.

Smash, crack, splat!

'Never mind the eggs,' said Alex. 'Go after Mops.'

Frankie raced away, with her parents close behind.

She caught up with Mops in the field, where Dillon had just fed
the cows. He was driving down a slippery bank when, to
Frankie's horror, the tractor slid out of control. It rolled and
landed upside down.

Mops crept to Frankie, shivering with fright.

'Good boy,' she said, grabbing his lead.
She hurried to the tractor.

A HOLIDAY TO REMEMBER

'Dillon's trapped!' she shouted to her parents.

Dillon had a broken arm and leg.

'He needs an air-ambulance to hospital,' Alex told Pete.

Pete rang the emergency services and called Rachel to tell her about the accident.

Frankie was first to spot the helicopter. The whirr of rotor blades was deafening as the pilot landed skilfully.

'We don't want you running off again!' Frankie said holding on to Mops.

'Well,' said her dad. 'Just for once, it was a good job he did. Otherwise you wouldn't have found Dillon so quickly.'

Frankie felt a twinge of pride.

Dillon was put on a stretcher and carefully lifted into the helicopter.

'Thanks!' he said. 'You saved my life.'

Next morning, they went to say goodbye to Rachel and ask how Dillon was.

'They fixed him up,' said Rachel. 'But it'll be weeks before he's driving the tractor again.'

'Who says nothing ever happens in the country?' said Alex.

Frankie rolled her eyes.

'Okay, Mum,' she said. 'I know I got that wrong!'

Then Frankie went to say goodbye to Florence.

'I'm going to miss you,' she said, stroking the donkey's soft, grey nose.

'Here,' said Rachel, handing Frankie a small package. 'Something to remind you of her.'

Inside was a framed photograph of Florence and a certificate to show that Frankie had 'adopted' her.

'Your mum and dad paid for you to adopt Florence,' said Rachel. 'The money helps us to care for her and the other donkeys we rescue. It costs a lot to keep them and pay our vet bills.'

Frankie was so happy she couldn't think of anything to say.

But she didn't need words. Her smile said it all.

As they drove home, Frankie told her parents:

'I've had the best holiday ever. I can't wait to come again!'

Free Range Eggs

One fine hen lived in a barn,

Laid her eggs all over the farm.

Ten in the orchard,

Nine in a sty,

Eight near an oak with a river running by.

Seven by the tractor,

Six in the hay,

Five in a field where the new lambs play.

Four in the cowshed,

Three by the gates,

Two in the yard where the sheepdog waits.

And one brown egg, safe from harm –

All by itself in her nest in the barn.

Bouncing Bed Bugs

There were once some bugs who loved to bounce. They particularly liked bouncing on beds.

On **Monday** night the bugs visited Billy the baker. He had to be up early to bake bread. But that night the bugs –

Bounced on his head.
Tickled his toes.
Bounced on his chin
and did a jig on his nose!

They kept Billy the baker awake, and he was much too tired to bake bread. His customers went away hungry. So Billy the baker shook out the bugs and said:

'No, no, no! Not in *my* bed. Off you go!'

On **Tuesday** night, the bugs visited Pippa the police officer. She was on traffic duty at the carnival parade next day. But that night the bugs –

Bounced on her head.
Tickled her toes.
Bounced on her chin
and did a jig on her nose!

Pippa the police officer had a dreadful night, and she was late for work. The carnival parade was held up in a traffic jam for hours! So Pippa the police officer shook out the bugs and said:

'No, no, no! Not in *my* bed. Off you go!'

On **Wednesday** night, the bugs visited Declan the doctor. He had lots of patients to see next day. But that night the bugs –

Bounced on his head.
Tickled his toes.
Bounced on his chin
and did a jig on his nose!

Declan the doctor tossed and turned, and he was late getting to his surgery. He kept his sick patients waiting and they weren't happy. So Declan the doctor shook out the bugs and said:

'No, no, no! Not in *my* bed. Off you go!'

On **Thursday** night, the bugs visited
Bonnie the bus driver. She had to
drive the children to school.
But that night the bugs –

Bounced on her head.
Tickled her toes.
Bounced on her chin
and did a jig on her nose!

Bonnie the bus driver couldn't sleep a wink for hours, and then she
overslept. The children were late for school and their teacher was cross.
So Bonnie the bus driver shook out the bugs and said:

'No, no, no! Not in *my* bed. Off you go!'

On **Friday** night, the bugs visited Paul the postman. He had a mountain
of letters to deliver next morning. But that night the bugs –

Bounced on his head.
Tickled his toes.
Bounced on his chin
and did a jig on his nose!

They kept Paul the postman awake and he put letters through the wrong
letterboxes by mistake. So Paul the postman shook out the bugs and said:

'No, no, no! Not in *my* bed.
Off you go!'

By Saturday, the bugs were running out of beds to bounce on. They flew around, looking for somewhere to stay. That night they found Patsy the park keeper. Patsy had to be up early to open the park. But that night the bugs –

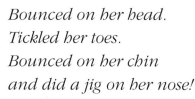

> *Bounced on her head.*
> *Tickled her toes.*
> *Bounced on her chin*
> *and did a jig on her nose!*

Patsy the park keeper couldn't sleep at all, and she was late opening the gates on Sunday morning. There was a queue of people waiting to come into the park. So Patsy the park keeper shook out the bugs and said:

'No, no, no! Not in *my* bed. Off—'

She stopped. Patsy the park keeper had a bright idea. 'What you need,' she said to the bugs, 'is your very own place to bounce. I may have just the thing.'

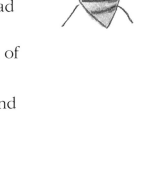

On Sunday afternoon, she went to her shed and took out an old trampoline. It had belonged to her children and hadn't been used for years. Patsy took it to the bottom of her garden.

'There. You can bounce away on that and not bother anyone.'

And the bugs *loved* it.

BOUNCING BED BUGS

They bounced on their heads,
They bounced on their knees,
They bounced over rooftops and flew over trees.
They bounced so high, right up to the moon,
Then bounced back home, before the clock struck noon.

'What a splendid idea!' said everybody when Patsy told them the news. 'Now we can all get a good night's sleep.'

And from that day on, Billy the baker, Pippa the police officer, Declan the doctor, Bonnie the bus driver, Paul the postman and Patsy the park keeper were never late for work again.

> Fe, fi, fo, fum!
> Look what
> I've found.

Buttons and
the Lonely Giant

One day, I was sitting by the Story Tree when I heard noisy footsteps.

Thud, thud, thud!

The ground shook. Someone had left a trail of large, muddy footprints and I wanted to know who. I decided to follow them. I hadn't gone far when I met Mole.

'Look what that clumsy giant has done,' said Mole. 'Trampled on my molehill and ruined my tunnel.'

'Did you see the giant?' I said.

'Not exactly,' said Mole. 'I heard stomping so I hid below ground. They say the giant has a dreadful temper and bellows like a bull.'

'That's scary,' I said. But I was still curious to see the giant for myself. I left Mole digging a new tunnel and continued on my way.

The footprints were enormous.

They led to a river where I met Duck. She was in a terrible flap.

Quack, quack, quack!

'The giant has broken the bridge,' she said. 'No wonder! Boots the size of barges.'

'Did you see the giant?' I asked.

'No,' said Duck. 'I hid in the reeds. Everyone knows giants like duck for supper. As many as ten at a time!'

I noticed that the bridge had a *few* damaged bricks – not quite as bad as Duck had described – so I hurried across.

The giant's trail led to a wood and there I met Squirrel.
Her teeth were chattering with fright.

'I'm l-l-lucky to be alive, Buttons,' she said. 'I was within a
whisker of being caught by the giant. Hands as big as houses,
you know.'

'Ah, so you got a good look?' I said.

'Almost,' said Squirrel. 'When I heard crashing I took cover.
You can't be too careful.'

Thud, thud, thud!

went the giant, somewhere up ahead. And with each crashing
step, the path shuddered beneath my paws. I was catching up…

Just then, Owl flew down. It was clear the giant had ruffled
his feathers.

'Phew!' said Owl. 'That was close.'

At last! I thought. *Here's someone who must know what
the giant looks like.* But I was wrong.

'Oh, I've no idea,' said Owl. 'I'm not silly! I flew away the
minute I heard those footsteps. They say the giant can swallow
a hundred birds in one go!'

Even this disturbing news didn't put me off. If anything,
it made me more curious about the giant than ever. Besides,
everyone seemed to know about the giant, except me! As I
hurried along the trail, I wondered if the stories were true. If
no one had actually seen the giant, how did they know? I was
keeping my eye on the footprints and not looking where
I was going, when – *'Ooof!'* – I bumped into something
blocking my way.

BUTTONS AND THE LONELY GIANT

At first, I thought it was a sack of potatoes. An enormous sack! I pushed, but it wouldn't budge. Then it started to rain – or so I thought – and blobs of water made puddles round my paws. I looked up. That's when I saw the girl's head. A giant girl's head!

She was sitting on the path, sobbing. I could see she was unhappy, so I took a deep breath and shouted:

'Hello! I'm Buttons. What's the matter?'

The giant girl looked astonished and stopped crying. Then she blew her nose so hard that the wind flattened my fur.

'You're not afraid of me?' she said. 'Everyone else is. They hide when they see me coming.'

'Er, they think you're going to eat them,' I said.

'Yuk! No way!' she said. 'I'm a vegetarian. I wouldn't hurt a fly, let alone eat one. I'd like to make friends, but no one will give me a chance. It's very lonely being a giant.'

'What's your name?' I asked.

'Ginny,' she said. 'Will you be my friend, Buttons?'

'Yes,' I said. 'Wait here. I'm going to tell the others.'

Mole, Duck, Squirrel and Owl were amazed when they heard about Ginny. They wanted to be friends too.

'Let's give Ginny a surprise party!' I said.

News about the giant spread quickly, only this time the stories were true. Everyone who came to the party saw how friendly Ginny was. She was careful not to tread on them – she did have very large feet – and let them ride on her shoulders for a sky-high view. So Ginny the giant made lots of friends and was never lonely again.

Look, we've got to the sea.

Everyone needs friends!

I'm glad it has a happy ending. No one should be lonely.

DOWN BY THE SEA

The Pop Pirates

Presley Grimshore lived with his twin sister, Maisy, on a pirate ship – The Mighty Mollusc. Mum and Dad were pirates. Uncle Redbeard was a pirate. And in her younger days, Granny Grimshore had been the most feared pirate-lady of the Seven Seas. Not surprisingly, everyone expected Presley to be a pirate too. Which was a problem because Presley had other ideas. But his parents were so busy treasure hunting they never had time to listen to him.

One day, when Presley and Maisy were visiting
Granny Grimshore, Presley told his granny all about it.

'I don't want to be a pirate,' he said. 'I want to be a
pop star. Play a guitar. Sing in a band.'

Granny Grimshore was horrified. Her face went
blotchy and turned a peculiar shade of purple.

'Bilge and barnacles!' she cried. 'Grimshores are
pirates. Not pop singers! You'll never get rich
twanging a guitar. Take my advice, Presley. Learn
to be a proper pirate like your wicked old granny.
I made a fortune plundering!'

She opened her bag, and gave two bright silver
coins to the twins. 'Spend it wisely,'
she told them. Then, to Presley:
'Work hard at school. Forget about
this band business.'

THE POP PIRATES

But Presley didn't forget. Next day on their way to Shipmates Pirate School, he asked Maisy what he should do.

'Well,' said Maisy, 'we always sing the same old sea shanties at school. Why not write something new? A pop shanty. I'll help you, if you like?'

'You're a genius!' said Presley.

Presley couldn't concentrate. He came bottom of the class at:

map reading,

deck scrubbing and

raising the Jolly Roger.

His teacher, Miss Fishwick, stamped her peg-leg in despair.

'You'll never make a pirate, Presley,' she said.

Which was exactly what Presley wanted to hear.

The last lesson on Friday was singing. Everyone gathered round, while Miss Fishwick plonked away on the piano. Her pupils sang badly out of tune.

'Stop, stop!' she cried. 'Go home and practise over the weekend. It's our concert on Monday. Your families will want a good sing-song.'

'You could sing your new song at the concert, Presley,' said Maisy on their way home. 'First, you'll need a guitar.'

'I'll buy one tomorrow,' said Presley.

THE POP PIRATES

Next day, the twins were greeted by shouts.

'Someone's stolen our treasure map,' yelled Dad.

'I'll bet my boots it was that thieving pirate Codface,' said Mum.

'We must catch Codface before he finds our gold,' said Dad.

'You can stay with Granny Grimshore,' Mum told the twins. 'Be there by teatime. Don't be late.'

As their parents set sail, Presley and Maisy hurried to the Harbour Music Shop. Presley chose a shiny, red guitar.

'I've always wanted to play the drums,' Maisy said, spotting a drum kit. 'And a pop band needs a drummer.'

'Great,' said Presley. 'Let's call ourselves The Pop Pirates!'

They bought the instruments with Granny Grimshore's coins.

'We must find somewhere to practise,' said Maisy.

'There's a cave near Granny's place,' said Presley. 'Smugglers used it a long time ago. Would that do?'

'Perfect,' said Maisy.

The cave was huge.

'*Yo-ho-ho!*' sang Presley, and his voice echoed.

Ho-ho-ho-hooooo!

Presley strummed his guitar. Maisy banged the drums. They both wrote the song. But as they were leaving for Granny Grimshore's, they heard gruff voices. Hearts pounding, the twins hid behind a barrel.

'In here, me lads,' barked a voice.

'Aye, aye, Captain,' said another.

'Give us a hand,' said a third. 'This chest is heavy.'

'That's because it's full of gold!' said the first. 'I told you Grimshore's map would lead us to the treasure.'

'*Codface!*' said Presley out loud.

'Sssh!' said Maisy.

Too late. Presley's echo came booming back.

Cod-cod-cod-faaaaaaace!

'Shiver me timbers!' growled Codface, kicking over the barrel. 'Who's there?' He found Presley and Maisy trembling with fear. 'Aha!' he said to his crew. Looks like we've got trouble-makers. Quick. Tie 'em up.'

THE POP PIRATES

Presley and Maisy watched as Codface and his crew sat round a campfire – drinking rum and enjoying a supper of shellfish. The pirates carelessly tossed their empty shells away, until one shell landed right beside Maisy. Grasping it in one hand, she used the sharp edge to cut through the rope. At last they were free. By now the pirates, drowsy from too much rum, were sprawling on the sand. The twins saw their chance to escape.

'Ready?' said Presley.

Maisy nodded.

'Let's go!'

When Granny Grimshore heard their story, she grabbed a cutlass.

'I'll teach Codface a lesson. Follow me.'

They charged along the beach, and in the moonlight, the once most feared pirate-lady of the Seven Seas looked a ghostly figure. Captain Codface got the fright of his life.

'Aaaarh!' he cried. 'Forget the treasure, boys. Run for it. *Run.*'

'Good riddance,' said Granny Grimshore. 'And don't come back.'

'Hooray!' cheered Presley and Maisy.

Somehow, they managed to take the treasure chest, guitar and drum-kit back to Granny Grimshore's.

Over a delicious supper of fish and chips, the twins told her about their pop band.

'Hmm,' grumbled Granny Grimshore. But there was a twinkle in her eye.

On Sunday morning, Granny showed Presley and Maisy how to send flag signals, to let their parents know all was well.

We've got the treasure!
See you later.
Love, Presley and Maisy xx

Then they practised for the concert, until Mum and Dad came to take them home. They were horrified to hear the twins had been captured by Captain Codface.

'They've been very brave little pirates,' said Granny Grimshore.

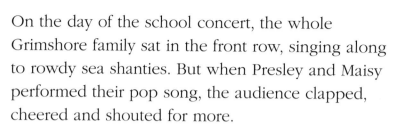

On the day of the school concert, the whole Grimshore family sat in the front row, singing along to rowdy sea shanties. But when Presley and Maisy performed their pop song, the audience clapped, cheered and shouted for more.

Even Miss Fishwick tapped her peg-leg in time to the beat. Everyone *loved* The Pop Pirates best of all.

Little pirates brave and cool,
Go to Shipmates Pirate School.
Set the sails and sing, Yo ho!
Treasure hunting, we will go.
Come, young pirates, do your best,
Find a long-lost treasure chest.
Then listen to your favourite band –
And dance to pop songs on the sand!

THE POP PIRATES

At bedtime, Presley thought of all the exciting things that had happened. He was confused about what he really wanted to be. A pop star or a pirate?

'It's fun being a pirate,' he told Mum sleepily. 'Especially when Granny Grimshore is around. But I like being in a band too.'

'Maybe you could do both?' said Mum. 'You too, Maisy?'

'Yesss!' said Maisy and Presley, punching the air. 'Pop Pirates for ever!'

'I'm glad that's settled,' said Dad. 'Goodnight, little pop pirates. Goodnight!'

Twenty Seashells by the Shore

20 **Twenty** seashells by the shore

19 **Nineteen** flags at the seaside store

18 **Eighteen** fishes, great and small

17 **Seventeen** seabirds on a wall

16 **Sixteen** crabs crawl side by side

15 **Fifteen** waves on an incoming tide

14 **Fourteen** turtles head for the sea

13 **Thirteen** nuts on a coconut tree

12 **Twelve** small kayaks cross the bay

11 **Eleven** kites fly on a breezy day

10   **Ten** deep rock pools, cool and clear

9   **Nine** sandcastles by the pier

8   **Eight** smooth surfboards, ready to float

7   **Seven** full nets on a fishing boat

6   **Six** big beach balls on the sands

5   **Five** young swimmers, holding hands

4   **Four** fun dolphins flip their tails

3   **Three** yachts race with wind-filled sails

2   **Two** yummy ice creams, pink and white

1   **One** tall lighthouse, shining bright

ICE & SURF

Doogle and the Runaway Egg

One day I was having fun, splashing about in the sea when, to my surprise, I saw an egg. It had washed up on the sand and was round-as-a-beach-ball-green-and-blue-with-ziggy-zag-stripes-and-spotty-dots-too.

The roly-poly egg went bowling along, quick as anything, And I did too!

When Toothy Thomas and Suzy Silver saw the egg – round-as-a-beach-ball-green-and-blue-with-ziggy-zag-stripes-and-spotty-dots-too – they thought it would make a super football.

Toothy Thomas and Suzy Silver ran after it too.

Before long, it rolled by the Seaside Café where Cherry the chef was making pancakes. When Cherry the chef saw the egg – round-as-a-beach-ball-green-and-blue-with-ziggy-zag-stripes-and-spotty-dots-too – she cried:

'Stop! I need one more egg for my pancake batter.'

Cherry the chef chased it too.

We flew after the speeding egg down to the harbour, where Finn the fisherman was in his boat. When he saw the egg – round-as-a-beach-ball-green-and-blue-with-ziggy-zag-stripes-and-spotty-dots-too – he said:

'Well, I never!' And he *caught* the egg in his net.

'Whose egg is it?' I asked.

'We wanted to play with it,' said Toothy Thomas and Suzy Silver.

'I wanted to cook it,' said Cherry the chef.

'Come with me,' said Finn the fisherman. 'I know who has lost this egg.'

We all climbed into Finn's fishing boat and went to sea.
Then, where the water was as deep as it could be,
a strange thing happened.

Whooooosh!

The egg – round-as-a-beach-ball-green-and-blue-with-ziggy-zag-stripes-and-spotty-dots-too – began to roll about. Suddenly – tap, tap, *crack*. It split open! And out climbed a tiny sea dragon.

An enormous monster burst through the waves. The boat rocked and we held on tight.

'It's Father Sea Dragon,' said Finn the fisherman.

'My baby,' he boomed.

'Sqwark! Sqwark!' said the baby sea dragon, flapping its wings.

'Sea dragon eggs are rare,' explained Finn the fisherman. 'I'm glad we saved this one.'

'Thank you,' said Father Sea Dragon. 'Mother Sea Dragon lost our egg when it was washed ashore in a storm.'

'Hooray!' everyone cheered, as the sea dragons swam away.

And I said:

'If I ever find another egg – round-as-a-beach-ball-green-and-blue-with-ziggy-zag-stripes-and-spotty-dots-too – I'll know who it belongs to.'

Finn the fisherman took us back to the shore, and Toothy Thomas, Suzy Silver, Cherry the chef and I all went home for our supper.

The Cat with Itchy Paws

There was once a cat called Cat — for a time he knew no other name — who travelled from place to place, looking for somewhere to live. Not just anywhere. Cat was seeking the purr-fect place to call home.

Even as a kitten he would wander. His mother once said: 'You have itchy paws, Cat. A cat with itchy paws is never satisfied. Before long, you'll leave to find somewhere new.' She was right. One day, Cat felt a twitchy-itchy feeling in his paws. So he said goodbye to his mother and set off.

For weeks, Cat roamed around town, catching mice and sleeping anywhere he could find. He dodged traffic on the busy roads, until the day his luck ran out. One morning near a block of flats, a cyclist came speeding down the road – fast. Cat froze.

The cyclist yelled, 'Out of my way!' but his back wheel caught the tip of Cat's tail.

'Miaow,' screeched Cat.

'Mia-ow-ow-ow!'

A little girl called Ali was playing nearby and ran to him.

'Poor cat!' said Ali, stroking his fur.

Cat had never been stroked before, but he liked the feeling. His tail hurt and the touch of her hand soothed him. Something told Cat he could trust Ali, because he allowed her to pick him up and carry him home.

Ali lived on the top floor of the tower block. Her father frowned when she brought Cat in.

'You know pets are not allowed,' he said.

'Oh, Dad,' said Ali. 'Can I look after him? *Please?*'

'Okay,' said Dad. 'But mind no one sees him or there'll be trouble.'

Cat tried to make himself at home. His tail soon healed, although it was bent at the end. He had a bed in Ali's room, and plenty of food. *Perhaps*, thought Cat, *this is the* purr-*fect place to live?*

But it wasn't. Ali played her music very loudly. And Cat couldn't see much from her window, because they were so high up. Most of all, he hated being indoors. Before long, Cat felt that twitchy-itchy feeling in his paws.

Time to be going. But how can I escape?

A chance came when a neighbour called to ask for some milk. Ali's dad went to fetch it and left the door open. Cat flew past Ali.

'Cat,' she cried.

But he didn't look back.

Cat trotted along a towpath, by a canal. He sat down to wash, near a brightly-painted barge – the Flora Dora. When he was perfectly clean, Cat looked around for something to eat. A movement caught his eye. Rat! It was running up the mooring rope, on to the barge. A second later, Cat pounced and caught it. The owners of the Flora Dora were watching.

'Clever cat,' cried Jake.

'We could use a rat-catcher,' said Jodie.

Cat stayed with them on the barge. He slept on deck and enjoyed catching rats. For several days Jake and Jodie steered the Flora Dora along waterways, taking Cat far from town.

Perhaps, he thought, *this is the* purr-*fect place to live?*

But it wasn't. The chug-chug-chug of the barge motor made his ears ache, and he hated the smell of engine-oil. In less than a week, Cat felt that twitchy-itchy feeling in his paws…

DOWN BY THE SEA

One afternoon, Jake and Jodie moored the Flora Dora near a farm. Straightaway, a herd of inquisitive cows came over to see them. Cat had never seen cows before.

'*Mooo,*' went the cows.

'Monsters,' Cat hissed. 'I'm going.'

He leaped off the barge and ran. Jake and Jodie were sorry to see him go.

Cat raced over a bridge and into a forest. He trotted along a path, until he reached a clearing where a woodman was chopping logs. Cat saw a campervan parked nearby, and noticed the door was open. He slipped inside. The campervan was neatly fitted with seats, a table and a bed.

'This will do,' Cat decided. 'The *purr*-fect place – at least for tonight.'

After helping himself to some scraps of food, he jumped on the bed, crept under the covers and went to sleep…

Much later, Cat woke with a start. Cat peered through a window. It was dark outside with only the moon and the van's headlights to light their way.

'Miaow,' Cat yowled. 'Miaow!'

The woodman screeched to a halt.

'You gave me a fright,' he said. 'Out you go!'

Cat walked for the rest of that night – up a hill, down another, across a muddy field and over a railway line. By morning, he'd reached the sea. Near the harbour, he saw a small wooden house. The front door was open, so he walked in.

A man was sitting at a typewriter. *Clack, clack, clack*, went the old-fashioned writing machine as his fingers tapped the keys. The man – a famous author – stopped typing when he saw Cat with his bent tail, torn ear and muddy paws.

'Hello,' he said. 'You look as if you've been on your travels. Would you like to live with me?'

Something told Cat they would soon be friends.

'Now, you must have a name. Do you like Gulliver?'

Gulliver purred. *At last*, he thought, *this is the* purr-*fect place to live.*

And it was. Well, almost. Gulliver found the *clack, clack, clack* of the typewriter a little annoying. Whenever that happened he went to the beach, stopping to dab at fish in the rockpools. But Gulliver always went home and never had itchy paws again.

Buttons Makes a Super Submarine

I was reading a story about a deep-sea diver. She was searching for a shipwreck, which had sunk with a hoard of beautiful jewels.

'I wish I could find the treasure!' I said. 'But I haven't got a boat.' Then an advertisement caught my eye:

Make Your Own Submarine
Don't delay!
Send for your Super Sub kit today.

'Just what I need,' I said.

I ordered one, and it arrived the very next day. The box was packed with an assortment of parts: a periscope, propeller and portholes. There was a page of instructions too.

DOWN BY THE SEA

It took me a week to fit the pieces together.

At last, when my Super Sub was ready, I set off.

Chug, chug, chug, went the engine.

Swish, swish, swish, went the propeller.

Drip, drip, drip, went a leak.

'Uh-oh,' I said. And caught the drips in a bucket.

When I was sure we had reached deep water, I set the controls to 'Dive'. Would the submarine work? I held my breath as I sank beneath the waves. Through a porthole I could see the strangest plants and sea-creatures. And some fierce-looking fish!

As we went deeper, I turned on a searchlight to see through the murky water. A few minutes later, the powerful beam picked out something on the seabed.

Swordfish

Kelp

Shark

Jellyfish

Seahorse

Coral
reef

A shipwreck! I was excited. Maybe I'd found the treasure ship. I saw a hole in the side of the ship so I edged towards it. Closer. Too close! A tentacle shot out and grabbed my Super Sub. To my horror, I saw we were in the grip of a giant octopus.

In a panic, I flicked a switch to 'Maximum Speed'. The engine roared. The propeller screamed and spun so fast – it broke off. But I'd caught the octopus by surprise. With a squirt of inky goo, it disappeared.

BUTTONS MAKES A SUPER SUBMARINE

Without a propeller the Super Sub was powerless, but we somehow rose from the depths. As we came to the surface, I peered through the periscope and spotted a dolphin, swimming round in circles. When I looked again, I saw her calf. Its flipper was tangled in a fishing net.

I wanted to help so I opened the hatch and climbed out. Mother Dolphin whistled in distress. Luckily, her baby floated alongside and I managed to release it quickly. The little dolphin turned a somersault, happy to be free again.

'Thank you,' said Mother Dolphin.

Then I told her I was in trouble too.

'We will tow you back to shore,' she said. 'One good turn deserves another.'

Although I didn't find a shipwreck full of treasure, I'd enjoyed an adventure at sea and helped some dolphins too. So my Super Sub was useful, after all!

HIDDEN VALLEY

Gordon the Ghost

Mr and Mrs Breezy and their children, Jonah and Violet, lived at Number Twenty-three, Windy Hill, Hidden Valley. Gordon lived there too — well, not 'lived' exactly — because Gordon was a ghost.

Long before the Breezy family moved in, Gordon had made himself at home in the cupboard under the stairs. When the Breezys heard rumours that Number Twenty-three was haunted, they were delighted and bought it straightaway. They thought having a ghost about the house was cool. So Gordon became part of the family.

whoooo-arrh!

At bedtime, Jonah and Violet were used to seeing Gordon in their room. He loved stories, even though the spooky ones gave him nightmares! Gordon was not like other ghosts. He was afraid of the dark. And he tried his best not to scare anyone – unlike another ghost he knew called Terrible Tina. She was always up to mischief. Her favourite trick was to fly about on a moonlit night, wailing. Which made people's hair stand on end.

One day, Terrible Tina floated through a wall at Number twenty-three and surprised Gordon in his cupboard.

'Call yourself a ghost?' she said. 'You're a wimp, Gordon. It's Hallowe'en tomorrow. Time for magic and mayhem!'

But before Gordon could ask what she meant, Terrible Tina vanished in a wisp of smoke.

Next morning, while they were having breakfast, Gordon overheard the family chatting about a Hallowe'en party.

'I'm going as a witch,' said Violet. 'I've got a cloak and a wand.'

'You'll need a pointy hat,' said Mum.

Jonah was dancing around in a skeleton costume.

'Do I look scary?' he asked.

'No more than usual,' said Violet.

'Ha, ha!' said Jonah.

'I've got tickets for the Ghost Train,' said Dad. 'It goes from the railway station at midnight.'

Just then, Gordon appeared in the kitchen.

'Hello, Gordon,' said Mum. 'You must come to the party too.'

'Yes,' said Violet. 'The Ghost Train will be super scary!'

'Have we got a ticket for Gordon?' asked Jonah.

'I think real ghosts ride for free!' said Dad.

Gordon hoped he'd be brave enough to go on the Ghost Train. Then he remembered Terrible Tina. He was afraid she'd spoil everyone's fun. But he made up his mind to forget his fears and keep a look-out for her.

That night, Mum, Dad, Violet, Jonah and Gordon set off down Windy Hill to the railway station. Soon, they were mingling happily with a crowd of children in fancy dress – wizards, witches, ghouls and ghosts. Gordon fitted in very well.

The station was decorated with pumpkin lanterns, bats and spiders. And there was crazy Hallowe'en food too. Violet munched a slime-green burger. Jonah slurped a monster jelly. Gordon drifted around, looking for Terrible Tina. Although he couldn't see her, he sensed she'd be up to no good.

The station clock began to strike midnight.
'All aboard,' cried Nigel the stationmaster.
Everyone scrambled to find their seats.
'Sit with us, Gordon,' said Violet and Jonah.
On the last stroke of midnight, Nigel waved a green flag.

Whooo-whooo, went the train whistle. Engine driver,
Kay, pulled a lever and the Ghost Train moved off. Before long,
they were clattering and rattling along the railway track
towards a mountain – and into a dark, dark tunnel…

Suddenly, to everyone's horror, hundreds of bats
came flying through the carriages.

'*Eeeeeek,*' screamed the children.

'*Oooo!*' moaned Gordon.

Terrible Tina appeared grinning
ghoulishy and laughing.

'Ooo-hoo-hoo-ha-ha-ha!'

Gordon was scared. But that wasn't all.

Something was wrong. There was danger ahead!

He flew through the tunnel – fast. Moonlight lit the rails. Rounding a bend, Gordon saw something blocking the line. A tree had fallen across the track. The train was thundering towards disaster. In seconds it would crash!

Gordon had to warn the train driver. But how? He whipped back to the engine and, in a blink, was inside the cab. Kay shrieked.

Gordon yelled: **'Stop! Stop!'**

Afterwards, no one could remember exactly what followed. Everything happened so quickly. The screech of brakes. The hiss of steam. The jolt as they came to a halt. One thing was certain. Kay had stopped in time. And no one was hurt.

'Where's Gordon?' said Violet.

'He disappeared while we were in the tunnel,' said Jonah.

'Well,' said Mum. 'You know Gordon. Here one minute. Gone the next. He'll be back.'

Then everyone helped to clear the tree away, so the train could pass.

Back at the station, Kay repeated over and over again:

'I saw a ghost. I know I did. It warned me to stop. If it hadn't been for the ghost…'

Nigel listened patiently.

'You've had a shock, Kay,' he said. 'And it *is* Hallowe'en. There are lots of ghosts about tonight.'

At that moment, Gordon reappeared. The Breezy family looked at him. They had a funny feeling he knew something about it. But Gordon didn't say anything. Not a word.

Later, when Gordon was in his cupboard, Terrible Tina came to see him. She surprised him by being friendly.

'You were soooooo cool, Gordon,' she said. 'You're not a wimp at all. I get up to mischief because I'm bored and lonely. I wish I could stay with a nice family like you.'

'There's room for two in my cupboard,' said Gordon. 'But you must promise not to scare anyone ever again.'

'I *promise*,' said Terrible Tina.

From that day Tina was never terrible again, and the two became very best friends.

Sam and the Amazing Bubbles

One evening, Sam was watching his favourite cartoon, Space Monsters, on television. His babysitter, Mina, was with him. Some awful aliens were chasing after the Rocket Kids in their spacecraft and catching up.

'Those monsters are a scary bunch,' said Mina. 'Look at their tentacles and claws.'

'I wish I was an astronaut,' said Sam. 'I'd love to zoom around in a spaceship.'

'Well,' said Mina, 'sometimes wishes come true.' She looked at her watch. 'Come on. Telly off. It's bath time. I've brought special bath bubbles.'

'What's so special about them?' said Sam, only half-listening.

'Not telling,' said Mina. 'Come and see.'

Sam knew better than to argue with Mina. Besides, he was curious about those bubbles. He pressed the 'Off' button on the remote and followed her up to the bathroom. While he undressed, Sam watched Mina pour bubble stuff into the water. He expected to see amazing bubbles, but the foam looked ordinary. He was about to protest when Mina said:

'Hop in, close your eyes and count five… backwards.'

Sam knew Mina could do magic. Maybe there was something special about those bubbles after all. He jumped into the foam, shut his eyes and counted:

'Five, four, three, two, one.'

Sam found himself inside a fantastic bubble spaceship! He was wearing a space-helmet and sitting at a control panel. He gave Mina the thumbs-up.

'Stand by for blast-off,' he said, as he reached for a lever and pulled it back.

Whooosh, zoooom.

The bubble ship shot through the bathroom window. In a blink, Sam was whizzing through space, surrounded by stars and planets.

'Wow!' he said. 'The universe is *big*.'

Sam soon discovered there was a lot of debris floating around in space. He dodged pieces of old rockets, and narrowly missed a tumbling meteorite.

Suddenly, a light on the control panel flashed a warning signal. An alarm buzzed –

Beep, beep, beep.

A voice boomed from a speaker:

'Aliens alert! Aliens alert!'

A flying saucer was approaching fast – way too fast. Sam saw two weird-looking creatures with tentacles, peering from the flight-deck window. They didn't look friendly.

'I'm off,' cried Sam. 'Time to fire the booster rockets.' He pressed a big red button. *Whoosh*. The bubble ship accelerated at a hair-raising speed. The aliens followed.

Sam fought to control his craft as it charged towards Earth.

The ground was coming up fast. The aliens were closing in.

Suddenly, Sam recognised familiar streets.
He could see his house. The aliens were right on
his tail as he steered for the bathroom window.
He was almost through it when the hatch of the
flying saucer flew open. A tentacle with a shiny,
sharp claw snaked out and took a swipe at Sam's
bubble ship – *pop!*

Sam landed in the foamy bath with a *splash*.
Mina shook soap suds from her hair and laughed.

'Hey!' she said. 'Watch out.'

Just then, Sam's parents came home.
They came upstairs to see what all the noise.
was about.

'I see you two are having fun,' said Dad.

'I've been flying in space,' Sam told him.
'In a bubble ship.'

'That sounds exciting,' said Mum. 'Where is this amazing bubble?'

'The aliens burst it,' said Sam.

'Hmm,' said Mum. 'Too much television, I think!'

They left Mina to get Sam ready for bed.

'I don't think Mum and Dad believed me,' whispered Sam.

Mina smiled.

'Well, I do!' she said.

Next morning, Sam got a surprise. There on the bathroom floor was a shiny, sharp claw – just like the one that had burst his bubble ship.

'Mina's bubbles really were special!' he said.

The Maze

A beetle, a snail and a centipede
Went into a maze to see,
Who could find the middle first –
The quickest of all three.

Beetle turned left,
Snail went right,
Centipede crawled ahead.
This way, that way,
Round and round.
'Will we *ever* get there?' they said.

Beetle ran west,
Snail slid south,
Centipede couldn't decide.
Right way, wrong way,
Up and down.
'We'll be lost *for ever*!' they cried.

Then…

Quite by chance, they *found* the middle,
And everyone had to agree:
'We have no idea how we got here,
Now let's go home for tea!'

Cabbage and the Flying Carpet

Not long ago, I found a carpet lying near my cabbage patch. How strange, I thought. I wonder who it belongs to? Just then, a white rabbit appeared. He told me his name was Marvin.

'Do you know anything about this carpet?' I asked.

'It belongs to Mr Moon the wizard,' said Marvin. 'It's magic. It played a silly trick on me. Horrid thing!'

Before I could ask any more, Marvin hopped away.

'A magic carpet, eh?' I said.

I gave it a pat with my paw. But the rug didn't budge.

I tried again. Not a twitch.

'Huh,' I said. 'There's nothing magic about this old rug. Marvin was having a joke.' But it looked soft. So I sat on it.

Which was a mistake.

At once, the carpet gave a tremendous shake, curled up a corner, then took off in a cloud of dust.

Swish, swoosh.

We flew so fast the wind whistled past my ears.
I clung on with my claws as we rose high into the
sky. In no time, we were flying over Hidden Valley.
When I dared to look down, I spotted a strange-
looking house in the forest. Next moment, the carpet
dropped, lower and lower, until we landed with a
bump at the door.

It was opened by Mr Moon.

'Ah, there you are, Marvin,' he said crossly.
'You naughty rabbit for whizzing off! I need you
for my magic show today.'

The wizard adjusted his glasses, to look at me more closely.
'Your ears are shorter than I remember…'

Uh-oh! I thought. *The wizard thinks I'm Marvin.* Quickly,
I told him who I was and how I'd got there.

'Oh, my stars!' said Mr Moon, wringing his hands. 'What shall I do? Children love my rabbit and hat trick. I should hate to disappoint them.'

'I'll help,' I said. 'If you teach me what to do?'

'Hocus pocus!' cried Mr Moon. 'We can try, Cabbage. But there's no time to lose. The show starts in two ticks. Come with me.'

So I followed the wizard back-stage, to rehearse.

'See this top hat?' he said. 'When I say the word – hop in.'

'What word?' I asked.

'*Abracadabra!*' he said.

And that was that.

✳

It was show time. I waited behind the curtain for my turn. I hoped I could do it, because the wizard was depending on me. The audience went, 'Ooo,' and, 'Aaah,' as Mr Moon performed each trick. Then I heard him announce:

'And now for my last spectacular trick, before your very eyes –'

He held the top hat upside down, to prove there was nothing inside. Then he covered the hat with a scarf, tapped his wand three times and said:

'Abracadabra!'

Oh, help, I thought. *Here goes!* I was bigger than Marvin so I struggled to fit inside. One leg. Two legs. It was a tight squeeze. Three, four… I could hardly breathe! And my tail was over the rim. Too late! Mr Moon whipped away the scarf and pulled me out.

'Ta daaa!' he cried.

'Ouch!' I said.

'Hooray!' cheered everyone. They were expecting a rabbit and got a nice surprise. It was the best magic show anyone could remember. Mr Moon was delighted.

'You saved the show, Cabbage,' he said. 'How can I thank you?'

'Just take me back to my cabbage patch,' I replied.

So we flew home on the carpet. Marvin was waiting there, and Mr Moon was very pleased to see him. After we'd said goodbye, the two went off happily together.

And that's the end of my story!

The Dancing Dinosaurs

One day, Little Diplodocus was playing near a pool when he heard an unusual sound. The little dinosaur went to investigate and found a band of musicians. They were playing a lively tune.

Clickety-click. Tum-te-tum. Ting. Boom-boom.
The music set the little dinosaur's toes tapping, and the conductor was delighted to see him enjoying himself.

'We're practising for the Jungle Ball tonight,' she told him.

'Can I come?' asked Little Diplodocus.

'Of course,' said the conductor. 'Everyone is welcome.'

He ran home to ask his mother:

'Can we go to the Jungle Ball tonight?'

'What nonsense!' she said. 'Dinosaurs don't dance.'

Little Diplodocus was disappointed. He went to tell his friend,
Little Stegosaurus, and they went to listen to the band.

Clickety-click. Tum-te-tum. Ting. Boom-boom.

The music set her toes tapping too.

Little Stegosaurus ran home to ask her father:

'Can we go to the Jungle Ball tonight?'

'Certainly not!' he said. 'Dinosaurs don't dance.'

The two little dinosaurs were sad and went to tell their friend, Little Triceratops. The three went to listen to the band.

Clickety-click. Tum-te-tum. Ting. Boom-boom.

The music set Little Triceratops's toes tapping too. He ran home at once to ask his grandmother:

'Can we go to the Jungle Ball tonight?'

'How ridiculous!' she said. 'Dinosaurs don't dance.'

The three little dinosaurs wondered what to do. They loved the music and wanted to dance. They went to tell their friend, Little Tyrannosaurus.

'Come and listen to the band,' they said.

Little Tyrannosaurus agreed and they all ran to the pool.

Clickety-click. Tum-te-tum. Ting. Boom-boom.

The music set Little Tyrannosaurus's toes tapping too.

'I have an idea,' she said. 'Let's dance together, right now!'

So they did.

Just then, Little Tyrannosaurus's father came looking for her.

When he heard the band and saw the little dinosaurs dancing, his eyes opened wide with surprise. The music set his toes tapping too.

'What fun!' he said. 'Dinosaurs *can* dance. I must tell my friends. We shall all go to the Jungle Ball tonight.'

And the dinosaurs danced and sang:

'Down at the pool by the light of the moon,
Dinosaurs dance to a toe-tapping tune.'
Clickety-click. Tum-te-tum. Ting. Boom-boom!

At the end of their Storytime adventures, Doogle, Buttons and Cabbage arrive home with a hat full of stories. They hang the stories, one by one, on the Story Tree ready to read again and again.

© Phil Glew

Georgie Adams

is the successful author of
over 70 picture books, gift
books, treasuries and early
readers, mostly for young
children. Georgie lives
in Cornwall.

Magda Brol

was born in Wrocław,
Poland. After the birth of
her two little girls, Magda
turned her passion for
drawing into a dream job.
Magda and her family live
in London.

First published in the UK in 2019 by Zephyr,
an imprint of Head of Zeus Ltd.

This paperback edition published in the UK in
2020 by Zephyr, an imprint of
Head of Zeus Ltd

Text copyright © Georgie Adams, 2019
Artwork copyright © Magda Brol 2019

9 7 5 3 1 2 4 6 8

A catalogue record for this book is available
from the British Library.

ISBN (HB): 9781788541732
ISBN (E): 9781788541725

Typeset by Louise Millar
Printed and bound in Spain by Graficas Estella

Head of Zeus Ltd
5—8 Hardwick Street
London EC1R 4RG
www.headofzeus.com

FSC
www.fsc.org

MIX
Paper from
responsible sources
FSC® C009279